Who'll Pull Santa's Sleigh Tonight?

Laura Rader

Christmas was just around the corner.
The toys were wrapped. The lists were checked.
Santa's sleigh was polished and ready to go.
"Let's visit the reindeer," said Santa to Mrs. Claus.

As they approached the stable, Santa called out:
"Hello, Dasher, Dancer, Prancer, and Vixen!
Hello, Comet, Cupid, Donder, and Blitzen!
Are you ready to fly?"

The answer was a loud . . .

"Goodness gracious!" exclaimed Mrs. Claus.
The reindeer looked miserable.

"We aw hab codes!" said Dancer.

"Poor deer!" said Mrs. Claus.

Santa rushed off to tell the elves.
"The reindeer are sick!
Who'll pull the sleigh?!" he asked.
"We need a backup plan."

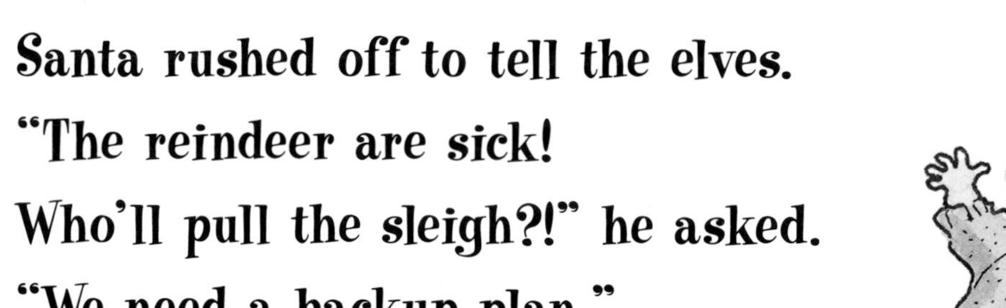

Santa paced up and down.
He scratched his head and looked serious.

Then he had an idea.
"We'll find stand-ins!"
he said.

Do you have what it Takes?
WOW!
Can you fly?!
I thought I'd wing it!
Auditions TODAY! in Workshop No.2
We don't accept bribes!
Ducks
Gators
Pigs

The auditions were announced.
A large crowd lined up to try out.

The performers were very unusual.

So were their acts.

None was right for the job.

I wish I'd thought of that!

Poor Santa.

I think he's upset!
Who'll pull the Sleigh?!!
Sweet Dreams & Flying Machines by J. Taylor
The Wright Way by

Santa went to his workshop.
He thought. He sketched.
He thought some more.
Then he had an idea!

"Here's my new plan!" said Santa.

There were a few grumbles and groans.
But Santa and the elves went to work.

They worked hard. They worked fast.
At last they finished.
"We did it!" shouted Santa. "Let's show Mrs. Claus!"

It was the **BIGGEST** idea Santa had ever had!

Santa prepared for a test flight.

The balloon went up, up, up.

The balloon came down,
down,
down.

The balloon was deflated. So was Santa.

"I'm all out of ideas," he sighed.

"I'll bring you a cup of hot cocoa," said Mrs. Claus.

Santa sipped the cocoa.
"Ahhh!" he said. "This always makes me feel good as new."
Santa and Mrs. Claus looked at each other.
I have an idea," said Santa.
"Do you think . . . ?"

"Yes! I DO!" she finished.

Santa and Mrs. Claus took a big pot of cocoa to the reindeer.

"I hope this works," said Santa.

Keep your fingers crossed!
Will it work?

The reindeer stopped sniffling.
They stopped sneezing.
They looked *much* better.
They were ready to fly!
"Hot cocoa saved the day!" Mrs. Claus said.

Best cocoa I ever had!
I like the candy cane!
I've got my bells on!
Come on! Let's fly!!

Everyone cheered as they flew out of sight.

Hot cocoa for all and

to all a good night!

This is delicious!
Ask an adult to help you!
Santa's Special Hot Cocoa
Makes 3 delicious mugs!
INGREDIENTS
2 Tbsp. cocoa
3 Tbsp. sugar
¼ cup hot water
1½ cups milk
a lot of tiny marshmallows (optional)
3 candy canes (optional)
Pour cocoa and sugar into a saucepan and slowly add hot water. Stir until ingredients are blended together. Bring mixture to a boil. Boil over medium heat for about 2 minutes, stirring constantly. Reduce heat and add milk, stirring occasionally, until entire mixture is heated thoroughly. DO NOT BOIL. Remove from heat and stir well. If you want, serve with marshmallows and candy canes. Add a big dash of Christmas cheer (for the best flavor)!

For my mother, who knew Santa very well.

With love, L. R.

Who'll Pull Santa's Sleigh Tonight?

www.harperchildrens.com

Library of Congress Cataloging-in-Publication Data

Rader, Laura. Who'll pull Santa's sleigh tonight? / Laura Rader.— 1st ed. p. cm.

Summary: When the reindeer get bad colds, Santa Claus wonders who will be able to pull his sleigh on Christmas Eve. ISBN 0-06-008088-4 — ISBN 0-06-008089-2 (lib. bdg.)

[1. Santa Claus—Fiction. 2. Reindeer—Fiction. 3. Sick—Fiction.] I. Title.

PZ7.R1155 Wh 2003 [E]—dc21 2002012739 CIP AC

Typography by Carla Weise

1 2 3 4 5 6 7 8 9 10

❖

First Edition